The contemplations of a
frantic mind

Dihan M. Struwig

You are free:

- **to Share** — to distribute and transmit the work
- **to Remix** — to adapt the work
- to make commercial use of the work

Under the following conditions:

- **Attribution** — You must attribute the work in the manner specified by the author or licensor (but not in any way that suggests that they endorse you or your use of the work).
- **Share Alike** — If you alter, transform, or build upon this work, you may distribute the resulting work only under the same or similar license to this one.

With the understanding that:

- **Waiver** — Any of the above conditions can be waived if you get permission from the copyright holder.
- **Public Domain** — Where the work or any of its elements is in the public domain under applicable law, that status is in no way affected by the license.
- **Other Rights** — In no way are any of the following rights affected by the license:
    - Your fair dealing or fair use rights, or other applicable copyright exceptions and limitations;
    - The author's moral rights;
    - Rights other persons may have either in the work itself or in how the work is used, such as publicity or privacy rights.
- **Notice** — For any reuse or distribution, you must make clear to others the license terms of this work. The best way to do this is with a link to this web page.

DEDICATION

To my family, and the love of my life, thank you for
sharing in my journey...

CONTENTS

ACKNOWLEDGMENTS

This book has developed over the course of a few years, and was made possible by contributions, as well as a wide variety of inspirations. I would like to acknowledge those who contributed passages and chose to remain anonymous. I would also like to acknowledge every artist and thinker mentioned in the book itself. There are various mentions of musical influences, as well as other influences of great minds and these people deserve a lot of credit for the inspiration they provided.

Chapter 1: Small towns and big dreams

There is something that we as human beings all share, something we are all driven by...

Needs, dreams and aspirations.

They have the power to consume our whole being, and the force to change the course of our entire life. But in order for this to make sense I need to share some background with you.

I am not sure when it all began, but things started to change about seven years ago. I am still not sure in which category I should place my decision, was it a need, dream or aspiration? All I know is that seven years ago I chose to leave the small town I grew up in, to chase that bright star on the horizon.

This small town was not one of those so see in the movies, where everyone knows everyone, where everything things seems perky, and with some weird serial killer living on the outskirts of town. No this was a pretty normal town, just outside the big city. Men would work in the big city in order to provide for their families, women would work to pay the bills. Kinds would attend school and partake in rebellious teenage behaviour. Times at home would be spent by parents fighting kids slamming doors and playing loud music. Evenings would be spent in front of the television with everyone enjoying a home cooked meal. On weekends teenagers would spend evenings at house parties, with few minor disagreements with parents about appropriate clothing.

As I said a normal small town with normal people caught up in the post modern mindset of consumerism, humanism and individualism. Seven years ago I was one of those normal teenagers in that normal small town. However I just completed high school and things needed to change. As I said I am not sure if it was a need, dream or an aspiration, all I knew was that I must get out of that town. Maybe it was the fear of being stuck there in the same old patterns forever! That created the desire to flee. Or maybe it was the words from a song by one of my favourite bands of the time, which inspired me to make a change. This band became the voice of the Afrikaans speaking youth of South Africa, and the words go as follow:

"'n Baie algemene mens, met baie algemene woorde in algeneme huis, kweek algemene drome. 'n Dosis pyn verdowers, op die ou einde van die dag, is dit seker maar al wat jou gelukig maak..."

Fokofpolisiekar- Monoloog in stereo

Maybe it is true that an average person in an average household cultivates average dreams…

I should not dwell on the past to long, but what is important is that I did get out. And seven years after I left I find myself sitting on a bench at the University campus in the big city.

This was the perfect place to sit with a few trees providing sufficient shade. Out of the way, and close to the chemistry building, and the fact that people assumed everyone in the area is science geeks, social contact was avoided. However it was one of the main routes across the campus which led to high traffic for which the big city is known.

As I put the disposable cup of coffee down on the bench beside me I look up and see the river of people that is flowing past me. I feel like a wild animal beside the river as I sit quietly in place and watch the stream flowing in the direction of the least resistance.

I have always been amazed by people and can sit for hours observing their behaviorisms and loose myself in my own thoughts. When I get lost in my thoughts like this it is like the timeless elegance with which a leaf falls from a tree into a rushing river below. This drifting process might seem timeless but as soon as the leaf hits the water it gets caught up in the flow of the river and is dragged along with the current. As streams flow into rivers and rivers into oceans and forms part of an astounding water cycle that sustains life in one form or another, we find ourselves in different stages of life as well.

I take a packet of cigarettes from my pocket, take one and light it up. I take a sip of coffee from the cup next to me to wash down the after taste of the cigarette. My quiet observations of the surroundings are disturbed by a young man asking if he can borrow my lighter. He is dressed in a black skin tight jean, a leather belt with a buckle the size of a fist and a t-shirt of some heavy metal band. His light brown hair is uncombed and covers most of his face, with his eyes hidden under a pair of aviator sun glasses. I hand him the lighter and after lighting his cigarette he hands it back to me. As I take the lighter from his hands he thanks me with the words "shots, dude". I simply give him a nod and he slips away in the current flowing past.

With another drag from my cigarette I gaze after this punk and notice how he stands out from the rest of the current that he is caught up in. As the character fades between buildings and the flow of people seem to quiet down a little, I realize that my time has come to swim with the current as well. I put out my cigarette and take the last sip of coffee, as I get up I fling a leather shoulder bag over my shoulder and start walking. I find myself amongst a group of students and the current will drag me along to my next class.

That is the stream I am caught up in at the moment, a student observing campus life between classes. When this is all done these students around me will probably flow into the next stream, find a job, get married, settle down and hope to reach the vast quiet ocean of retirement. Once there they will bask in the sun until their time comes to make the journey to sky and hand over to the next generation that will rain down and start their life cycle through the rivers of life. I am hoping to escape this cycle at some point and be one of those people that stand out from the rest of crowd, but for now my only escape is my thoughts.

The mind is a wonderful part of our being and is capable of holding large amounts of information. It has been proven in psychology that the human capacity for learning is unlimited. Information is gathered over the years as we flow through the cycle of life, and is gathered from every possible situation that we find ourselves in. Questions are one of the many ways in which information can be gathered, it might even be the main source. The answers to some questions might determine the course in the complex lifecycle of each person.

The one question that each person faces at some point in life is a question that might be as old the lifecycle itself, one question without a universal answer...

What is my purpose, my destiny?

Although my course seems to be set, I still find myself caught up in the ebb and flow of this life cycle. The question that has been ringing in my mind for the past few minutes is... What am I doing here?

***

It was a Sunday morning and Clive was dressed in the way he usually finds himself dressed. He feels a little out place, dressed in worn dirty sneakers, black skin tight jeans and a t-shirt of one of his favorite bands, The Ramones. The question that is on his mind does not concern his choices in studies, or at least not now. Currently his thought lingers on his current life circumstances, and the age old questions of purpose and destiny.

Clive brushes the hair out of his face to reaches for the cigarette behind his ear and starts walking towards a group of people. The three guys he is walking towards are all dressed in pale color shirts and jeans. The only way he can distinguish them from each other is by their hair styles and the different colors of their pale shirts. As he reaches them the question arises again, what am I doing here? He tries not to show that he feels out of place, and as he noticed them smoking he forces out the words, "can I borrow a light please?"

One of the young men dressed in blue jeans, and a pale green shirt, reaches into his pocket and hands Clive a lighter. Without even looking at Clive he continues his conversation. From the way that he is built Clive can assume that he works out, and his appearance is important to him. His hair is an ash blond color with white highlights, short and neat on the sides and the top is combed upward in spiky, out of bed look. His pale green shirt is tucked in into a slight bootleg, dark blue jean, and a neat sharp pointed black shoe that shines so much Clive can see his own reflection in them.

-"So I am thinking of changing my course this semester" he said. He stops talking for a moment to take the lighter Clive is handing back to him, looks and Clive and says, "Peter by the way."

-"Thanks, I'm Clive" he responds.

-"The blue shirt is Vaughn, and that's Frank", Peter said as he pointed towards the other two guys. Vaughn was slender built and tall, with dark brown hair neatly cut and combed in the traditional wet look. His pale blue shirt was also tucked in, in a stone washed straight leg jean with an ankle high brown boot. Frank on the other hand was short and bit chubby but not over weight. His hair was longer than and not as neat as those of the other two, not combed either.

Clive nods in greeting manner, and turns towards Peter, "so you are planning to change courses?"

-"Yeah, I'm switching to accounting, I don't think I'm cut out to be lawyer", Peter said and takes a drag of his cigarette.

The other two guys smiled.

- "you weren't cut out to be a journalist either", Vaughn said. He turned towards Clive and asked, "And what are you studying?"

-"Physics", Clive replied.

This conversation made Clive feel a bit more at ease and the uncertainty started to fade. He didn't feel so out place anymore, and he felt normal for pondering questions about purpose and destiny after hearing that Peter experiences something similar.

-"We should go in, their starting", Frank said.

Almost instantaneously Clive is reminded about the question he asked himself before he was caught up in this conversation. He turned towards the large doors and as he looked at the people going in, dressed in their smart-casual outfits, the uncertainty returned. He grew up in a Christian home and believing in a Creator God explained the design of the natural laws he finds in his studies. However Clive always felt religion was for the week and stupid. With the hope to find answers for other uncertainties in his life he follows the crowd into the church.

With the hope of feeling some sense of belonging and experiencing a form of transcendence, Clive takes a seat close to the back of the church. The tremendous size of the building itself contribute to a sense of transcendence. It is a long building filled with row upon row with wooden benches. The high ceiling is decorated with elaborate paintings, that seems to date back to the renaissance and in the front of the building a large stained glass depiction of the crucifixion. The rumble of the people struggling to find a place is amplified by vast open space in the building, and the light that beams through the stained glass picture dances across their faces. As everyone settles down the silence is overwhelming, creating an atmosphere that is awe inspiring and the experience itself feels sanctifying to Clive. The silence is broken by music and choir voices, which sounds better that any recording he has ever heard due to acoustic of the building.

As the sermon starts Clive is accustomed to his surroundings by now and his attentions begins to wonder. This was not exactly what he expected but has been a wonderful experience. With his attention drifting around the room, he notices something out of the corner of his eye. This person seems somewhat out of place but appears to be comfortable, almost as if he is at home. He estimates the man to be around his mid twenties, dresses in a slight bootleg blue jean that is torn around the ankles and knees. Clive assumes the jean is ripped at bottom due to his bare foot walking, but can't explain the torn knees except for age. He is also wearing a white long sleeve button shirt, with the sleeves rolled up about a third up his arms; it is not tucked in. From the way the shirt fits Clive can see that he is well built but still slender. His dreadlocks are neatly tied back with a hair band, exposing his pierced ears. As he reaches into the shoulder bag, placed next to him on the bench, Clive notices that he has several bangles on his one arm.

He removes a book from the bag that seems to be as old as the paintings on the roof of the building, and he opens it to follow the scripture reading of the sermon. His relaxed body langue and his overall appearance make him seem relaxed to Clive, but that is not why his attention remains fixed on him. Clive knows that he has seen the guy before, but cannot recall the memory, and his thoughts remain fixed as he tries to recall the memory. Clive is snatched back to reality as the person next to him hands him a basket filled with money, and Clive just passes it on. He realizes that he has not heard a word from the sermon and focuses his attention to listen to the final benediction. The sermon is finished and people start heading for the doors. As Clive sat at the back he is out quickly and hangs around outside for while. He notices the man in the torn jeans walking out, and is still struggling to find the memory of where he has seen him before. As the man reaches into his shoulder bag and takes out a cigarette, Clive's memory is refreshed. He decides to walk closer and try to start a conversation but has no idea of what to say. He finds himself next to the man and still searching for words. He looks up and they both stare at each other speechless for a brief moment.

The silence is broken when the man in the torn jeans utters a few words to guy standing in front of him in silence.

-"You need a light, dude?" the man in torn jeans asks Clive with a mocking tone in his voice.

-"Uhmmm, yeah if that can be accompanied by a smoke" Clive respond awkwardly.

-"I haven't seen you around here before, first time?" he said.

-"Yeah" Clive responds not quite sure how to continue the conversation, but being a student falls back on the easy conversation.

-"Are you studying?" Clive asks not quite sure of what answer he is expecting.

-"Yes I am, but I saw on campus, what are you studying?" he responds.

-"Physics" Clive answers and his answer is followed by another brief moment of silence. The silence is broken by another question.

-"So are you leaving satisfied today?" followed by a gesture that implies he is enquiring about Clive's name.

-"Clive, and not really" the responds follow.

-"Yip, except for the building I don't find it to be life changing either Clive. But what did you come here to find?"

-"Answers, I guess?" Clive answers, with an expression of confusion on his face.

-"Well it's your question, so only you can find the answer. But I have to run we'll talk again Clive. Keep up the search, oh and you can call me Slash". He simply leaves and Clive is left standing in front of the church with even more question that he began with.

Although he did not find the answers he came here looking for, he feels a sense of satisfaction. Clive has more questions than he started out with but a new journey has begun for him. Feeling more confident he realizes that although he has not felt a sense of belonging, finding people that share the same feelings overshadows the loneliness.

As Clive begins to walk away from the church building, the character he just spoke to lingers in his mind. Why does he feel so drawn to this guy? Is it due to his maturity and that he might have insight to life that he still needs to learn? Or is it because he seems to be different from the average people that surround him? Or maybe there is some natural law of physics that has drawn them together?

***

I have always been fascinated by physics and science, and found that some human relationships can be described in the terms of the laws of physics. Sir Isaac Newton contributed greatly to the world of physics and I have found that his third law can be used to describe conflict situations sufficiently.

Newton's third law: When two bodies interact, the forces on the bodies from each other are always equal in magnitude and opposite in direction.

For instance if a disagreement arises both parties defend their point with equal force, and no motion towards a resolution is present. There are many more examples of how science can contribute to human relations, thus the keen interest in science.

My interest in science and physics was present for as long as I can remember. As a small boy, in a small town, Albert Einstein was my idol. My inspirations was found in the fact that he was misunderstood for the majority of the time, and that he persisted in that which he believed. When he was able to get his point across, he was able to change the way in which the people of the time thought. Not only did he change the way in which people thought he was also able to change the world, and contribute to the wars of others. He was one of those people that stood out from the crowd, one of those people that I dream to become.

As I sit in my usual place on campus my thoughts dwell on my youth. Today I am not paying attention to the behaviorisms of the people around me, and I rather contemplate my noble causes. As I sit and contemplate quietly I sketch my childhood hero, and I wonder if I have lost my dream...

The contemplations of a frantic mind

As I young boy who found his inspiration in Einstein, I used to have a similar causes. I used to dream up a large lab with glass tubes running everywhere. I will be dressed in a white lab coat with, glasses and long hair that is going in every direction. I would scribble a few extremely difficult formulas on the black board and then turn to the glass tubes, turn a tap or two, and poor some new chemicals into the one of the jars that is boiling and smoking on the counter. It was not long before these fantasies turned into reality and I was running between the garage and kitchen. The garage would be where I wore the safety glasses and work in secret, in the kitchen I would be mixing and cooking, then run back to garage to mix everything and see if it explodes, dreaming of one day discovering something that will change history.

I did not realize it at the time, but these fantasies became mixed with reality and made me a serious geek. Soon I found myself seeking friends with similar interest, to such and extend that I found myself on chess team of the school. It was not long before I was exposed to a new fantasy world with my new friends, a world with foreign worlds, aliens and wizards.

This new world of fantasy and friends to share it with gave me a tremendous sense of belonging; suddenly I was part of something greater. My 'lab' made me a non-expendable part of the group, and my projects went from failing explosion to a fortress of geeks. Making use of the tools in the garage I was building pretend laser shooting hand guns, and x-wing battleship. My creations made the 'Star Wars' role playing a tangible experience instead of just a fantasy world with fingers in the shape of guns. I was slowly becoming a combination of Albert Einstein, the 'crazy' scientist, and George Lucas creator of the Star Wars fantasy world. I was dreaming of becoming the next great revolutionary that would change the way in which we view the world.

The dream to become the next great revolutionary however was not the main goal at the time, as I was caught up in teenage desires. Firstly I would need to become the hero, to win the heart of a girl of course. Her name was Charlene and she sat across from me in the fourth grade math class. She was not a princess like princess Leia, her hair was not dark and bound in two doughnut shaped figures next to her head. She had a small figure with long blond hair, and spoke in a light high pitched voice. We lived in separate worlds, while I was battling strange creature on the school playground, she was caught up in the pop culture, consumed by the girl group of the time. While her and her friends would practice songs and dance moves I would fly by in my spaceship and be struck with passing comets of ridicule.

If my extra ordinary battle skills and bravery would not impress my sheer intellect would surely do the trick. After school I would return to fortress of glass tubes and the big black board, to improve my math skills. Although I was only in the fourth grade I would attempt seventh grade math on my own and as soon as I mastered it Charlene would surely be impress in the math class.

My brilliant plan was not successful and only led to me being bored during the math period, an effect that lasted all through high school. If bravery and intellect was not the answer literature was my next great venture, but the mastering of that skill had to wait until the seventh grade. I wished away the time and in what seemed like a moment my fantasy world and science experiments became distant by the seventh grade with only vague memories remaining.

It was only in the seventh grade that we had a prescribed book to study for English, and I could join the poetry club. I became so caught between poetry and literature studies that I only had time to leave an occasional note on the desk of my dream girl, but the influence of the pop culture was to strong. The words of the Back Street Boys were the only words that could soften the heart of a seventh grade girl.

It was then that I awakened from my comatose state on the bench of the University campus to see Clive walking by. I decided to invite him over for a smoke and maybe some light conversation on science and its applications on life. This was a desperate attempt to relive the childhood dream of being a revolutionary scientist and maybe some conversations of difficult natural laws would connect me to the small boy inside of me. As he came over I put away my sketching pad in my shoulder bag and took out my packet of cigarettes and the lighter. He sat down beside me and as I hold the open pack of cigarettes he removes one and places it in his mouth. I hand him the lighter and take a cigarette myself, as he hands me back the lighter and I light up the cigarette I say: "So what's new?"

-"Not much, you?" he responds.

-"Nothing new" I reply.

-"So you never told what it is that you study, at church" he curiously asked.

-To which I responded "at the moment not what but whom".

As he leans forward he rests his elbows on his knees he looks at me with confusion in his eyes. I take another drag from my cigarette and as I exhale I point towards a young man, which caught my eye, locking up his bicycle in front of the chemistry building. He has an athletic body structure probably from the cycling, and long hair bound in pony tail.

-I put my hand down and say "look, his t-shirt is from a rock climbing club, and he is wearing cross trainer shoes. His shorts show his toned calves, so it's clear that he is adventurous. He is going into the chemistry building so it is safe to assume that he is studying chemistry."

- To that Clive responds, "And?" with more confusion in his voice.

- I continue, "So, in his choice of studies he has to challenge the way in which he thinks as well as the way in which he does things. This has obviously impacted his live and he is challenging his physical abilities as well. Isn't stereotyping fun?"

-He looks at me with a slight smile on his face and says, "Sure, and this is what you do to pass the time?"

- To that I responded, "Well, yeah".

-"So you sit hear judging people by what they wear and how they act?" Clive asked with a tone of amazement in his voice.

-"Think of it as science, studying a particle and predicting the reaction when in contact with another particle", I responded.

-Shaking his head from side to side, he let out a chuckle and said, "Ok, let me give it a go".

As we sat on the bench smoking I was astonished with some of the observations Clive made. Over the next few weeks this became a regular pass time activity for the two of us. When we would see each other on campus we would share a smoke as some laughs as we observed the students around, we even went so as far to compile a set of notes on our observation, placing people into categories. With my interest in science and Clive knowledge we would even pair up people according to their behavior, making this activity a scientific study. This activity did not connect my present reality and childhood dreams, but at least for a few moments a day I was connected to the dream of becoming a revolutionary.

PEOPLE SKILLS 101

The CEO:

Normally the leader of the group
Field of study: Economics / Finance

- Self assured !
- Task orientated
- Strong willed
- Seems mean
- hard headed
- unemotional

HUGE EGO

❋ NEVER CONFRONT DIRECTLY

MOTIVATED BY PERSONAL GAIN

$

The geek:

Classically the quiet collected member of the group.
Field of study: science/risk management

- Calm
- Thinks before acting
- Sarcastic
- Fearful
- Uninvolved
- Tolerant

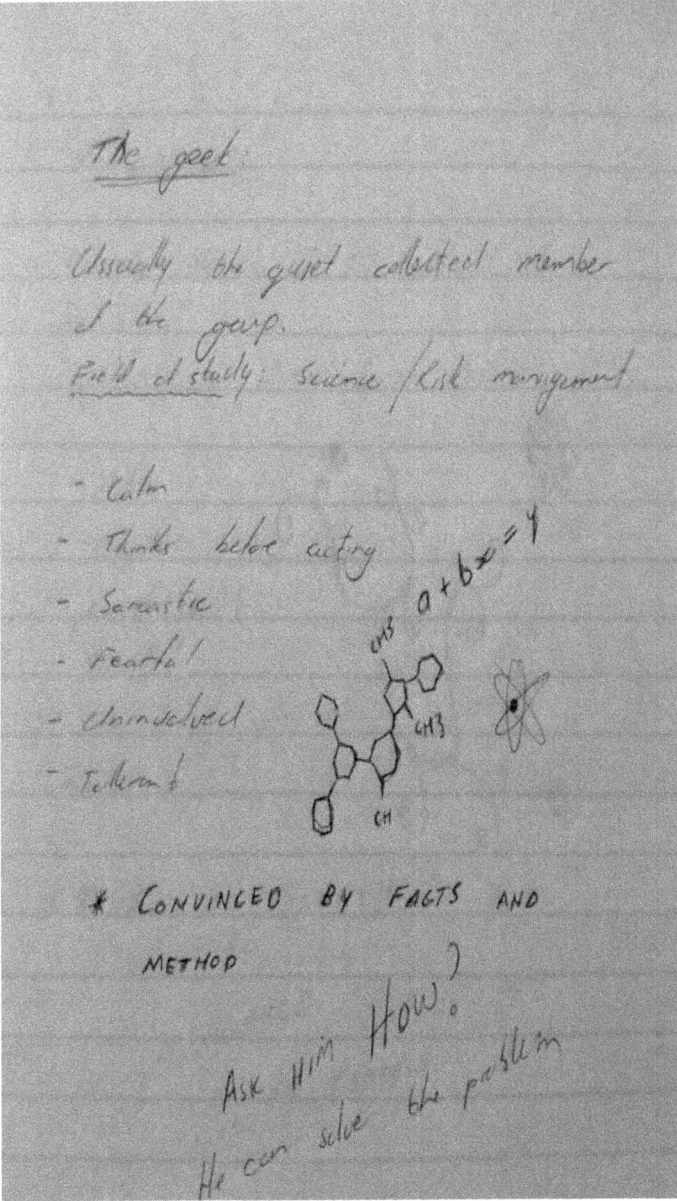

$a + bx = y$

* CONVINCED BY FACTS AND
  METHOD

Ask HIM How?
He can solve the problem

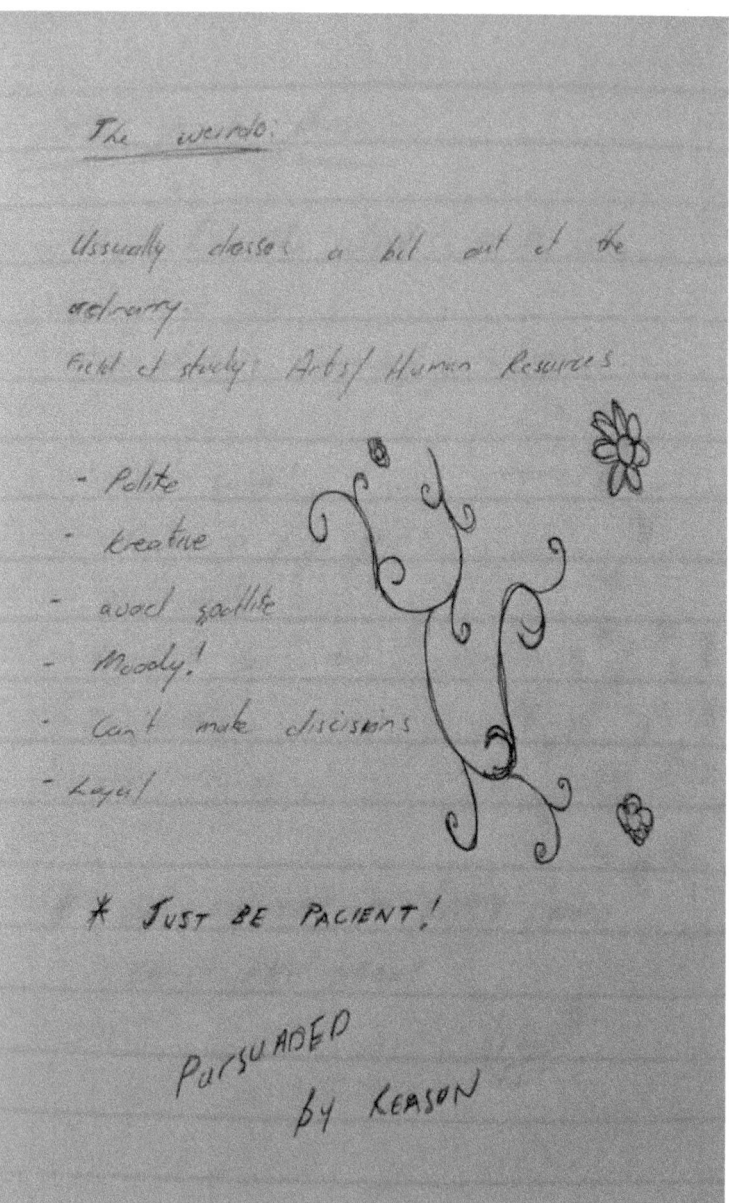

The weirdo:

Ussually dresses a bit out of the
ordinary.
Field of study: Arts/ Human Resources.

- Polite
- kreative
- avoid spotlite
- Moody!
- Can't make dicisions
- Loyal

* JUST BE PACIENT!

PARSUADED
by REASON

26

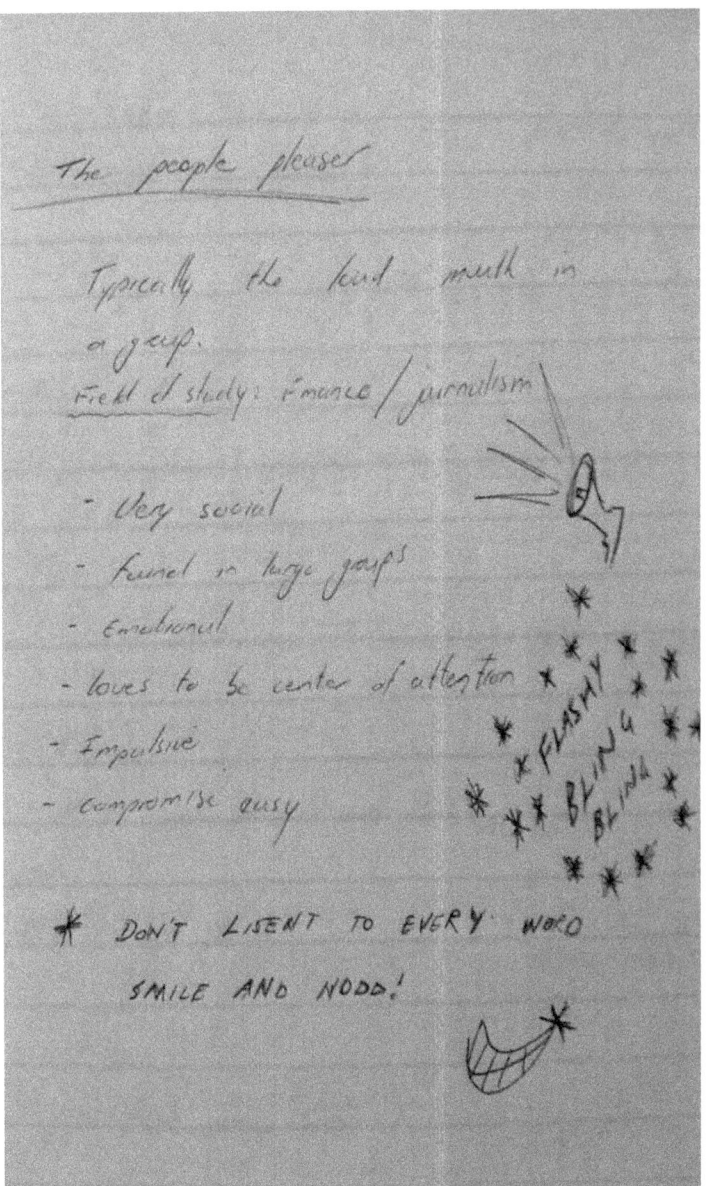

The people pleaser

Typically the kind much in
a group.
Field of study: Finance / journalism

- Very social
- Found in large groups
- Emotional
- loves to be center of attention
- Impulsive
- compromise easy

★ DON'T LISENT TO EVERY WORD
    SMILE AND NODD!

The relationship between me and Clive grew into an unexpected but welcome friendship. Our conversations on campus, and the study of human behavior that we conducted, was a pleasant escape from my contemplations on life and my youth. We seemed to have a lot in common and I discovered a friendship that I did not have since my days in primary school. Our scientific studies evolved into a sharing of the hidden secrets of the fantasy worlds.

It has been a while since I talked with someone about the marvels of Star Wars and computer games. It was not only, Star Wars, computer games and science that formed part of the intricate discussions between me and Clive. We disagreed and debated about the most influential people in the world of science and fantasy, from Isaac Newton to Albert Einstein, through to Stanley Kubrick and George Lucas. It was not long before our debates turned to the world of music with long discussion on bands from the Beatles, to the Ramones and Black Sabbath.

We shared common interests but we were different people. It was these differences that kept the friendship alive, and where I regarded myself to be more of a thinker, Clive was a practical person. I could contemplate the artistic nature of music, Clive would explore the possibilities. And in essence it is our thoughts that separate us from the animal kingdom, and I did not feel like a wild animal beside a river anymore. The connections we make with people make us part of lager picture in the world. The ebb and flow of life is greater than students rushing between classes, and from our childhood dreams to our destiny contributes to our lifecycles.

Chapter 2: The metal scene

I could spend hours listening to music and contemplate its artistic nature; it is this characteristic that gave me my nickname. The nickname was given to me one night at a bar as I was sharing my thoughts on the skills of lead guitarists. As I was wearing my Guns & Roses t-shirt, the people with whom I was sharing a drink nicknamed me after the guitarist of Guns & Roses. This was an identity that I would embrace, and it was also the identity through which Clive knew me.

Although I did not agree with Clive on a variety of musical issues he still acknowledged my good taste in music. Clive and I were engaged in our normal pass time activity of studying human behavior on campus when we started to discuss music. The discussion began as we were observing the students and noticed an attractive girl passing by. It was at that moment that Clive spontaneously began to sing the words of a Counting Crows song.

"...Mr. Jones and me tell each other fairytales and we stare at the beautiful woman. She's looking at you; oh no, no she's looking at me..."

Counting Crows – Mr. Jones

After we shared a laugh, Clive's singing led to us talking about the band that he formed part of. He was the drummer of an indie rock band named The Faceless. The name was fitting because as musician they are given a voice to express their opinions and feelings in a way which most people will never be able to. This was probably why I envied musicians; they can remain faceless but still be the voice of the people. There was that and the fact that a band can attract a crowd that usually included women. I had the opportunity to observe this nature of music as The Faceless was playing this weekend at a local bar and Clive invited me to go to the show.

Friday approached and I headed down to The Dragon, the local bar where The Faceless was performing. The Dragon was an old house that was converted in to a bar. In front of the bar there were still a few trees reaming from the old garden, lit by green spot lights.

Under these trees were wooden benches and tables, making this a popular spot as it was away from the busy bar counter and stage.

As I passed through the garden area I reached the wooded deck porch and the entrance to the bar. After I paid the cover charge I stepped into the first room, here there were leather couches and coffee tables, giving the bar a lounge atmosphere. I passed through to the next room, which had the largest crowd due to the bar counter. The room was dark except for the dramatic antique chandelier that lit the bar area. The counter was a dark solid wood counter with silver detail, and silver bar stools. The walls were covered in black and white pictures of every kind, from famous people, historical figures and popular brands.

The room to the left was the pool room, which I avoided, and proceeded straight to stage area. The wall on the right side of the stage was broken down leading to another garden area, with an outside bar. It was there that I found a place to sit, and planned to enjoy the show, I also had a good view of the area in front of the stage to observe the crowd.

There was no stage warmer act; instead a DJ played some deep house music in the background, to keep the crowd alive. I haven't seen anyone familiar yet so engaged in my favorite pass time activity observing the crowd. The Dragon was a place that drew the entire social outcast community, from punks, Goths through to the geeks and the simply those that are bored with clubs. I was disappointed that I did not bring a note book, but this did not keep my thoughts from drifting.

As I observed these marginalized people that filled the bar, the first thoughts was of my childhood heroes. Those influential people that changed the course of history on their own, they were also marginalized at some point. Was this the kind of place that people like Albert Einstein and Chè Guevara would hang out on a Friday night? If this was the gathering place for the socially marginalized the people I meet here could be next great revolutionaries.

The house music began to fade; I got up and walked to the bar. To avoid pushing through the crowd again I got myself two beers, before The Faceless began to play. As I returned to my seat Clive and the rest of the guys took the stage and began to play their first song.

As the distinct sound of The Faceless ran through the speakers my eyes are drawn to the reaction of the crowd. Some were clearly there for the music alone and others simple to get drunk and enjoy a night out. As I observe the crowd I am struck with contrast between the people I see here and those that I see at church.

Like Clive, most people attend church to experience a sense of belonging, transcendence and the need to serve a greater purpose. These needs or even desires are universal and one of the unifying factors that holds the church community together. I am not sure if it is because I am surrounded by people that might change the world, but I feel more at home here than at the church. Here among the socially marginalized I experience a sense of honesty, and acceptance. It is as if all of the goals that the church community is aiming for are present here, love, unity, no pretense and probably the potential to change the world. At yet both these places address the same deep needs people experience. I decide to part from my thoughts and just enjoy the music with the crowd.

A few days later I found myself between classes and I got myself a take away coffee, and made my way to the chemistry building. As I reach my favorite bench I light up a cigarette, took a seat and placed the disposable cup next to me on the bench. I recall the memory of the evening at The Dragon, and my thoughts began to dwell on the influences of music.

As I begin to contemplate the influences of music on my life, I notice that heavy metal has probably had the strongest influence. I try to recall the exact memory of when I was first exposed to the genre, with no success; I only get so far as the seventh grade.

It was during the seventh grade that I gave up hope on chasing the girl of my dreams. I was the nerdy guy and she was the popular chick, and it was during that time that I experienced heartbreak for the first time. I did not realize it would be the first of many, and the feeling consumed me at the time.

I was a member of the student council at the time and it was there that I started to make new friends. One of these new friends was Cindy, she was not as attractive as Charlene and I was surely not going to fall in love with her. It was Cindy that rescued me from the fantasy world of the nerds and exposed me to an entirely different world, a world of rebellion. It was with Cindy that my journey into the world of heavy metal began, as she exposed me to the band Korn.

It was when she invited me over to her house one weekend, when it all began. We were a few friends playing truth and dare, and it was during this game that I had my first cigarette. As we explored the forbidden things like smoking and alcohol, that the '*follow the leader*' album of Korn was playing in the background and I associated with some of the words immediately.

I was not long after I experienced heartbreak that I heard the music of Korn, and I associated with songs like freak on a leash.

"Feeling like a freak on a leash, feeling like I have no release. How many times have I felt disease? Nothing in my life is free..."

Korn – Freak on leash

This new genre of music changed my life, as I experienced a form expression I did not know before. It was as if these words were my own, and expressed my every feeling exactly. From rage to anger, through to disappointment, this was the music for the socially marginalized. But it was not only negative feelings, there were songs describing success and accomplishment, there were even song for love and lust. It was not long before I discovered hard rock and heavy metal for every mood I experienced. This was a journey in the musical world that I often still take part in. As a thinker I often find it difficult to express my thoughts, feelings and opinions, and I find it much easier through the artistic nature of music.

As I sit there on the bench by the chemistry building I struggle to recall the extent of my friendship with Cindy. I cannot remember the way she looked or even how much time we spent together, I don't even know what happened to her after the seventh grade. However if it was not for her I might still be stuck in my fantasy lab, so I had her to thank for that. As I put out my cigarette, I also despise her for exposing me to this habit.

I decided that this shaping part of my life needs to be documented in some form. Although I have not spent a lot of time contemplating this period I still needed to make some form of note. As I struggle to express myself I decided that this needs a lot more contemplation. As this period consisted of the artistic nature of music something artistic would be appropriate. I reach into my shoulder bag and take out my sketching pad and pencil. As the band Korn was the band that started this journey of rebellion, I decide to sketch one of their album covers to capture and remind me of the contemplations of this period. The album cover that I decide to capture artistically was the album cover of Issues, the first Korn album that I bought.

***

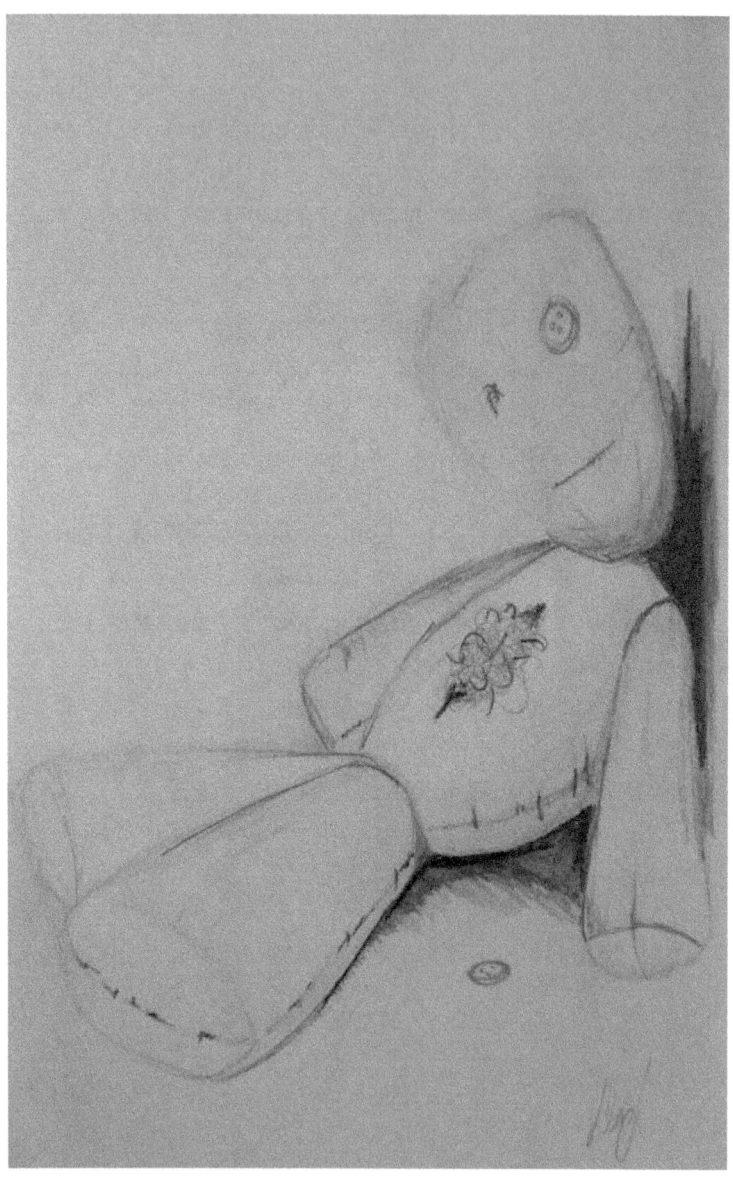

When I started to think about my journey into rebellion again, the seventh grade was only the beginning and it lasted for a few years. By the time I reached high school I was a changed man and part of an entirely different world from the fantasy world of primary school.

I attended one of the leading high schools of my small town, one that excelled in sports, academics and cultural activities. These were all of the activities that I took part in during primary school and continued as well as part of my new identity. My academic and leadership qualities of primary school landed me in the class with all the 'stuck up' over achievers.

 I was not an excellent sportsman but partaking in sports landed me between the jocks, and my choice in music and rebellious attitude made me acceptable to the rebellious teens as well. The fact that I knew people in every social group made me quiet well known. My geeky friends from primary school new all the places in the school yard were other people never came, which gave my rebel friends the opportunity to smoke at school and not get caught.

I enjoyed this part of the journey a lot and I was exposed to new realities that would shape me. Not all of these experiences were beneficial for the future but it was experience none the less. House parties became a regular activity for me, smoking and drinking was acceptable behavior. However it did not stay with smoking and drinking, it was not long before I experimented with marijuana and having sex. I was living the rock star dream of sex, drugs and rock & roll, with all the popularity that came with it. As most revolutionaries had some elements of a rebellious nature, I viewed these experiences as servicing a greater purpose.

So much has changed since then, but after attending the show of The Faceless it stirred up a desire to relive the glory days. Over time I began to spend more time with Clive and met the rest of the band members as well. I was intrigued by the lifestyle of one of the members, his name was Steven and he was the lead guitarist of the band.

Steven was taller than average and very slender making him seem almost anorexic, and had long curly hair which seems dirty and tangled. He reminded me of an early rock star like Aerosmith, maybe even a member of the Guns & Roses. He didn't shave very often, and he dressed in clothes that look like it has been handed down to him from his parents. His favorite outfit was a pair on straight leg; stone washed jeans with leather boots and a sleeve less t-shirt. Although he looked as if he was a homeless person he was very smart and was studying music and philosophy at the university. It was not long before he joined me and Clive on the bench at the chemistry building on campus, and he and interesting views on people and their behavior.

Steven was living the hardcore rocker lifestyle and it was not long before our usual gathering spot was no longer stimulating enough. We had to move our place of gathering to somewhere where beer was available and our view obscured by clouds of hanging smoke. So instead of meeting on campus between classes we moved to the Dragon to have a beer, a few smokes, and felt free to have alternative views on life. Steven's high intellect always resulted in interesting conversations. It was during one of our regular visits to the Dragon that our conversation once again turned toward people and music and the alternative views of Steven broadened the perspective of Clive and me.

With Steven's keen interest in anthropology and religion the conversation progressed toward how heavy metal as been stereotyped and dismissed for centuries. As Steven was a metal enthusiast he has also been stereo typed and dismissed which provoked strong feelings in him. He especially felt disappointed and fostered a deep anger towards Christianity. I am not sure if this is due the influence of heavy metal or the strong judgment from the church on this music and him, however it was enlightening. I gathered all my courage and was able to ask Steven about his feelings about the church but I would never have anticipated the response I received in return.

Steven began: "Well in order to answer the question properly I would have to start with the history of rock and heavy metal. For me and probably the rest of the world it all began in the early 50's with the American *Bill Haley & the comets* that made rock music popular. At that point in time rock music was popular and acceptable, and resulted in the fame of Elvis Presley.

However the music changed and evolved with times and by the 60's the picture started to change. In the 60's we see the rise of the British band *the Beatles* who created the legendary album *Sgt. Pepper's Lonely Hearts Club Band*. This era also produced *the Rolling Stones*, not only were both these bands British but they are both famous for their psychedelic rock music. Another band that made contributions to psychedelic rock was *Pink Floyd* and they made other contributions as well. The most griping contribution was the introduction of theatrics to elaborate performances. It was not the psychedelic element of these bands that caused controversy but that it formed part of drug revolution that swept across the world with LSD as the most mentionable. The use of LSD combined with the psychedelic elements of rock music changed the world.

It was this revolution that caused rock music to be largely dismissed by society. Not only did this result in the now popular warning labels on cd's but also resulted in religious groups launching their revolt against this kind of music, claiming that it caused a new birth in Satanism. And so beginning in the 60's a revolution was started that has endured until today.

Since the 60's rock music became more aggressive, rebellious and confronting. This is a genre of music that challenges performing arts as seen with Pink Floyd, and it challenges society and normal behavior, and challenges religion. And it is this challenging element that has drawn me to this genre of music since I was in high school."

Steven paused for a brief moment, took a sip of beer and lit a cigarette. He looked at me and said, "What was the question again".

This conversation was so educational at the moment I was wondering how he was going to get from a history of rock to his religious feelings. Without hesitation I replied, "What is your opinion on the church and Christianity?"

-"Oh Yes, as you gather by now I am fascinated by rock music and its evolution, and I could continue for days, but that will not answer your question. As I have already mentioned, rock music was marginalized due the rebellious nature of the genre as well as the drug revolution it accompanied.

According to me most rock star and the listeners have deep rooted questions, which is a sign of intelligence. These questions usually goes against what society would consider as acceptable and thus results in rage, anger and rebellion. I myself have question about the standards of society and I am discontent, and therefore my love for the genre of music. As I result of my feelings, questions and my choice in music I have often been frowned upon by the church and believers, and I have been one of the spiritually marginalized. For many years this grieved me and I had strong feelings against the church, however I have looked past the reactions of the people. So to answer your question clearly, I do not hate the church or believers, I hate the narrow minded view and restrictions on questions and therefore I choose not to associate with them."

This was an interesting answer, and I could relate to some of the feelings Steven expressed towards the church and its believers. This was not uncommon and for my involvement with the church I have seen a variety of people hurt in a similar way either by the church or its believers. As Steven expressed such strong feelings concerning the church I chose not to reveal my devotion to him at this point in time. I was

not the only moved by Steven's answer and I could see
on the expression on Clive's face that he was also
intrigued by the answer, almost as if Steven was
talking about him. From his reaction I realized that in
the future Clive would be spending a lot more time
with Steven, and this would become a shaping time in
his life, and who knows where this path will take
him…? I decided that it was time for me to go, and as
I stood up to leave and Clive said that he was going to
stay behind and catch up later.

***

As Slash left I told him that I was going to stay
behind, and catch up with him later, I was intrigued by
Steven and wanted to know more of whatever he
knows. As he left, the conversation continued for a
while longer on rock music and its influences over the
decades, there was so little that I knew. The only
reason I was into that kind of music is because I
experienced a form of expression I did not get
anywhere else. From that moment on I started to look
up to Steven as some kind of sage of wisdom, and I
felt like the young apprentice hero that is destined for
greatness, if I follow his wisdoms…

Chapter 3: A Hero is born

It was a pretty normal Wednesday and I woke up early with the intention to attend a few classes later on during the day. I haven't smoked weed since a was in high school but since, hanging out with Steven, and less with Slash, I took it up again and decided to roll myself a joint with my morning coffee. I got out of bed to switch on the kettle, went to my room to put on some music, and rolled a joint. I went outside to smoke, and came back inside, made my coffee, and went to my room.

As the mellow feeling of the high kicked in I lit up a cigarette, and put on some Japanese anime to watch, it seemed I can only keep up with the subtitle when I'm high. I loved anime because of the fast action and intense emotions expressed in the cartoons. That morning I was watching *Bleach*, which tells the story of young man who receives the power to become a

Shinigami or Soul Reaper. With his new power he has to defend the human race from evil spirits and guiding the deceased to the afterlife.

In my dazed high I got carried away in the emotions portrayed in the series, and before I realized it I had missed most of my classes. But at that moment nothing seemed more important; I smoked a few more joints, and watched the series with enthusiasm. I felt a strong connection between myself and the main character of the series, and I had to figure out why. Overwhelmed and charged with emotions I got up to make some coffee to calm me down, and I decided to smoke another joint just to take the edge of with the coffee.

As I was sitting outside smoking and sipping away, like lighting it struck me that there had to more to life… As the Shinigami in the series I too must be destined for greatness and in order to discover my destiny I had to embark on an epic journey of self discovery. This journey will shape me into the person I need to be, I will find the love of my life and the world would never be the same again…

The only way for me to embark on this journey is to have someone to guide me, someone with wisdom, and someone who, in some sense of the word, is already a hero.

Before I could embark on this journey I had to use what I have already learned, and I definitely had to take notes. Maybe one day I could turn these notes of mine into an epic novel, of a hero, embarking on journey of self discovery. On this journey the life lessons he learns can be depicted as great monsters, which result in tumultuous battles, this can be filled with emotions. Through these battles the young man becomes a hero, and like all true heroes he could save a damsel, which in turn becomes the love of his live...

That evening the journey for me to become a hero began, note book in hand, I was ready to see the wise sage Steven. When I arrived at his flat I could see the smoke bubbling out of the windows, with the usual crowd hanging around. Steven's flat was a ground level bachelor's pad. When entering through the door, you enter a small hallway with the bathroom on the left hand side, and after the hallway the room opens up to the open plan flat. The kitchen on the left hand side, separated from the rest of the flat by a counter. Past the kitchen you enter the main living area with the desk with the computer on the left hand side and a sleeper couch on the right. That was basically the only furniture that he owned. The flat was poorly ventilated by one window and the smoke use to hang in the poorly lit flat like in a club. As I entered I saw the kitchen counter looking like a buffet counter of drugs, and Steven sitting on the couch with his guitar. He played amazingly and people gathered around him like disciples at the feet of an oracle. I was here to learn and observe as I did many times before with Slash but he was not here, and this was not his usual crowd. I helped myself to a joint and sat on the ground close to Steven so that I could hear him playing and I took out my note book to draw a few sketches.

I was just completing my sketch when I noticed her, as she came closer to sit down beside me, and I knew I've seen before. Her name was Stephanie and she was in my physics class, I've had an eye on her for a while, but I didn't know she knew Steven and was into drugs. This new revelation changed things, and made me even more interested in knowing her. She had long blonde hair, hanging about in the middle of her back, and she wore it loose. She was slender built, and short, you couldn't see much of the rest of her body as she dressed in loose fitting clothing. She didn't wear any make-up, but there was something about her face that was beautiful. Her dress style was more hipster than anything else, and so was the way she thought and talked. She was something different; unlike anyone I have ever seen or even dated before. All of this made me think that she might be the damsel I was looking for, but I was not ready to reveal this to her.

As she sat down beside she asked: "what are you up to?"

My response came out as: "I am being inspired."

-"Inspired?" She said with a sense of amazement in her eyes.

-"yes, music speaks to the heart." I said and handed her my note book.

She looked at the sketch and said: "This is good, does it have any meaning?"

I lit up a cigarette, looked at her and responded: "The eye is the window to the soul, and the man standing there, the inner man, is not a clear image…"

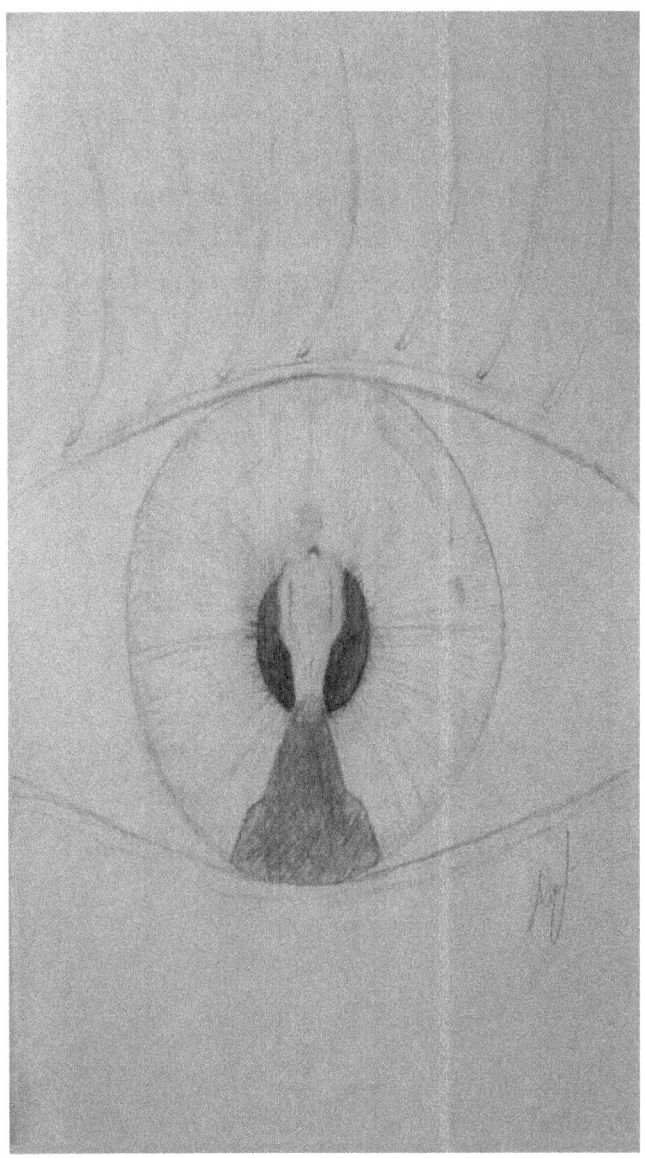

With that said the conversation ended there and from the corner of my I saw Steven taking note of what I said and put down his guitar. He came closer and stood over me with his right hand extended to help me up from the floor. He didn't say a word until we reached the buffet counter of drugs. He reached down and picked a small piece of paper, about the size of my finger nail, and handed it to me.

He took one himself and said: "chew on this and enjoy."

He walked over to the sound systems, put in on, and he played some psychedelic trance and dimmed the lights some more. Then he walked over to Stephanie, sat down beside her, and put his arm around her. I was not sure what to make of what just happened, but as I viewed Steven as sage, I trusted his judgment and admired his boldness. I was not long before I experienced the full effect of my first LSD trip and just sat down and let my mind be controlled by the drug...

The next morning I was not quite sure what to make of my experience of the previous evening, all I knew was that I needed a joint to mellow out. As I made the journey back home, I knew that the journey of becoming a hero has begun and there was no turning back now. The walk home allowed me to contemplate the effect of the LSD but all I could wrap my mind around was that it was amazing, not only did it alter reality but altered my mind as well. This new experienced influenced the way in which I viewed my journey of becoming a hero.

When I arrived home I switched on the computer to play some music and lay down to sleep of the drugs of the previous evening. As I laid on the bed, the music started to play and it was *Wheatus*, one of my favorite bands, filling the air.

"He's got the dirtiest shoes that I've ever seen, chew on blunt wipe his but with a magazine, smoking his crack wash it down with some gasoline… …Leroy is mojo man…"

Weathus – Leroy

I slept for a while to sober up, just to start this cycle all over again, smoke a joint, watch anime, go Steven's place and get wasted, and classes and studies just faded to the background. The only alteration in this cycle would be the faces at Steven's place, or maybe a change of venue, but the proceeding remained the same.

The repetition remained the same until one day I had the opportunity to spend some time alone with Stephanie and this was an opportunity I was not going to allow to slip away. That day I met her at the university sports grounds, which was empty and quiet at the time. It was in the afternoon as I slept the whole morning as usual and we would go to Steven's place together from the sports grounds. We met at the top of the stands, and sat together, it was not long before she broke out the joint. As we sat together with smoke rising and we stared out across the wide open field, she struck up a conversation.

-"Clive, I want ask you something about the night we first spoke."

-"Sure, don't hesitate", I responded.

-"I felt you looked at me in differently from the way you looked at the other girls that where there, is this true?"

-"I didn't think you noticed, but yes, I felt attracted to you."

-"I am glad to hear that Clive, because I have already noticed you a while ago in physics."

With that reply I was overwhelmed, here is a girl I noticed a while ago, and she did the same. I haven't been on this journey very long and I was looking for a damsel, and here she might be sitting right next to me. I was not sure how the journey was going to turn out but it seems that it will be going my way after all.

-"Stephanie, I am not sure what you are saying, but if you noticed me, and I have noticed you, don't you think we should give it shot? Me and you?"

-"Well now, this sudden, but I am sure we can give it a try."

With all that said we headed for Steven's place to continue our usual routine, of getting smashed, with the only difference that we where together. I was slowly becoming the hero; all I needed now was to gain some wisdom and experience from Steven the wise sage.

That evening at Steven's place the music was loud, and there were people lying around everywhere. As me and Stephanie arrived we were met with a look of surprise, as we were handed the first joint of the evening. After we had our smoke, our path separated for a while and I decided to gain some wisdom from Steven and expose my journey to him.

-"So Clive, what is up with you and Stephanie?" Steven asked.

-"Well it seems that we have noticed each other a while ago, and decided to try something. I think she might be the one."

With a slight grin on his face Steven did not respond to my statement, and instead turned towards the computer. He selected a song, and as it started playing he got up from his chair and walked away. The lyrics of the song began to ring in my ears as I watched him walk away.

"...But I can't seem to end, these images, haunting looks like hell. So to Carole plead silence, weak hands are calling..."

Chevelle- Panic prone

Amazed by his response I watched confusingly as he walked over to Stephanie and put his hand around her waist. This shocked me to my core, I felt betrayed and it felt like my heart is being ripped out of my chest. I watched as he whispered something in her ear, and went to sit on the coach. I was deeply confused by what just happed, my conversation with Steven was not over when he stood up, and what I just witnessed provoked me with anger.

I realized that this might me a declaration of war to which I had to respond. Steven might not be aware of my journey as a hero yet, neither that I looked to him for guidance, but he was not stupid. He might just be aware of more than I realize, and this might be my first battle as a hero.

As I took a moment to think about what has just happened I lit a cigarette and stared across the room at Stephanie. If Steven was planning a battle, the song he chose was his declaration, to which I had to respond if I accept. As I was looking at Stephanie, she smiled at me, and I decided that this was worth fighting for.

After all I am a hero she is my damsel, and the wise sage might turn out to be an enemy...

Still sitting by the computer, where Steven left me, I put down my cigarette down and started looking for a song that will set this battle in motion.

"I could be mean, I could be angry, you I could be just like you. I could be fake, I could be stupid, you know I could be just like you…"

Three days grace – Just like you

Thinking about her smile, and the look in her eyes which I did not understand, I was overwhelmed by my feelings for her. If I was going to win her heart in this battle I would need to expose my true self to her. So I decided that I would sketch from my heart and expose my softer caring side to her. This sketch would show her that I am serious and would like to share in an intimate relationship, where we can be exposed and it would be okay. When I show the sketch to her I will have the opportunity to talk to her and sweep her of her feet to a place where hero's and damsels share in destiny together.

Motivated and inspired I decide to sketch from the heart...

The contemplations of a frantic mind

Filled with satisfaction about the sketch I just completed, I decided that there have been enough emotions in this evening and it was time to relax. I stood up from the desk with the computer and walked over to the kitchen counter. I went and stood next to Stephanie, put my arm around her and kissed her on the cheek. I looked at the variety of drugs that are as usual, displayed like buffet on the counter.

I was not one for drugs like cocaine, or ecstasy, and decided to stick to LSD, not knowing that tonight this drug will change my life and the way I viewed the world...

After taking my hit of LSD I went to sit on the couch and let the drug take over. I sat quietly leaning into the couch as I observed the people, drifting off to a dazed state, and bright visual hallucinations. As I watched the people around, it played off as scene in a theater for the deranged. My attention drifted towards the guys in the corner of the room, and my ear caught their conversation...

-"Dude, are you seeing this?" the one said in slow almost whispering voice.

-After a few seconds the reply came; "Wow man, it's like, like, I don't know?"

After staring at the ground for a few minutes they burst out laughing.

Across from me in the room, stood a girl with long black curly hair, slender built in blue jeans and white t-shirt. She was just standing there staring at the picture on the wall with head slightly bobbing to the beat of the music playing.

The whole room was full of people walking up and down smoking, with the smoke hanging like a blanket over the room. Whenever two of them would bump into each other they would stop, and engage in a brief conversation before carrying on with the meaningless parade.

I was sucked in by this parade of the deranged, and whenever someone would sit next to me on the couch they would hand me a cigarette. I was so focused on the theatrics going on in the room I did not engage in any conversations. It was then that my eyes caught Steven again, and there was something different to the way he acted, as if he was above the parade. He was cool, calm and collected, taking part in the parade but seemingly somehow disconnected from it all.

He saw me looking at him, and he had that same grin on his face as previously, as if he was planning his next blow in our battle. He was standing at the kitchen counter taking part in some ritual of the deranged to get as high as possible. He stopped what he was doing and started walking through the room, whenever someone would bump into him who would engage in a conversation with the same detached atmosphere surrounding him. When he finally made it through the room he went and sat at the desk in front of the computer, and started scrolling through the songs. After he made his selection he swung the chair around, making eye contact with me, and giving slight nod. He engaged the conversation that was going on around him, and taking a cigarette from one of the guys next to him.

The lyrics of the song he selected struck with a blow almost snapping me out of my dazed state….

"… Your life is burning faster, obey your master! Master! Master of puppets are pulling the strings, testing your mind and slashing your dreams…"

Metallica – Master of puppets

As the song pounded on my ear drums, the drugs took over and going down a spiral of revelations. Steven noticed the anxious expression on my face, and came over to me, handed me a smoke and crashed into the couch next to me. We didn't speak, but I knew I was out of my league; he was the king of this hill. He was the master of the deranged puppets pulling the strings in this theater. This was not a battle, he is not going to be dethroned by an upcoming hero, and I was to become a puppet in theater.

After taking the cigarette from him it was time for me to make my exit, otherwise he was going to break me right there. Like a wounded soldier, in a foggy forest battlefield, I stumble around trying to find a way out of this madness…

The next few weeks were a downward spiral of confusion, as I was being consumed by my dreams and aspirations. I thought that in order to change destiny I was to become a hero, with personality traits that were desired by common folk, an empty dream that should rather remain fantasy…

I was beaten, struck down! And all that remained was for me to be the fallen hero, with lost dreams, giving himself over to addictions to calm the deep sorrows of falling in battle. My studies of physics only contributed to the confusion as the time and became one fuzzy void. My daily routines turned into getting high, going to classes, going to the local bar, destroy the bitterness I felt, and the song lyrics would ring in my ears…

"...you used to beg me to take care of things, and smile at the thought of me failing. But long before, having hurt, I'd send the pain below..."

Chevelle - send the pain below

It was one messy cycle, where the pain drove me to alcohol and drugs, the alcohol and drugs causing me to remember the pain. Instead of getting lost in my own thoughts as I did so many times before, I got lost in darkest place of them all,

Pain.

Loneliness.

Feeling Lost...

Life had no more meaning, and the harder I looked the less I found. I was studying physics to understand the working of the universe, but even this became a trivial pursuit. I used to find meaning in art, literature and music, but the sense of misdirection was to consuming. Knowledge was no longer feeding the desire for meaning, and beauty, and going to class seemed senseless.

The contemplations of a frantic mind

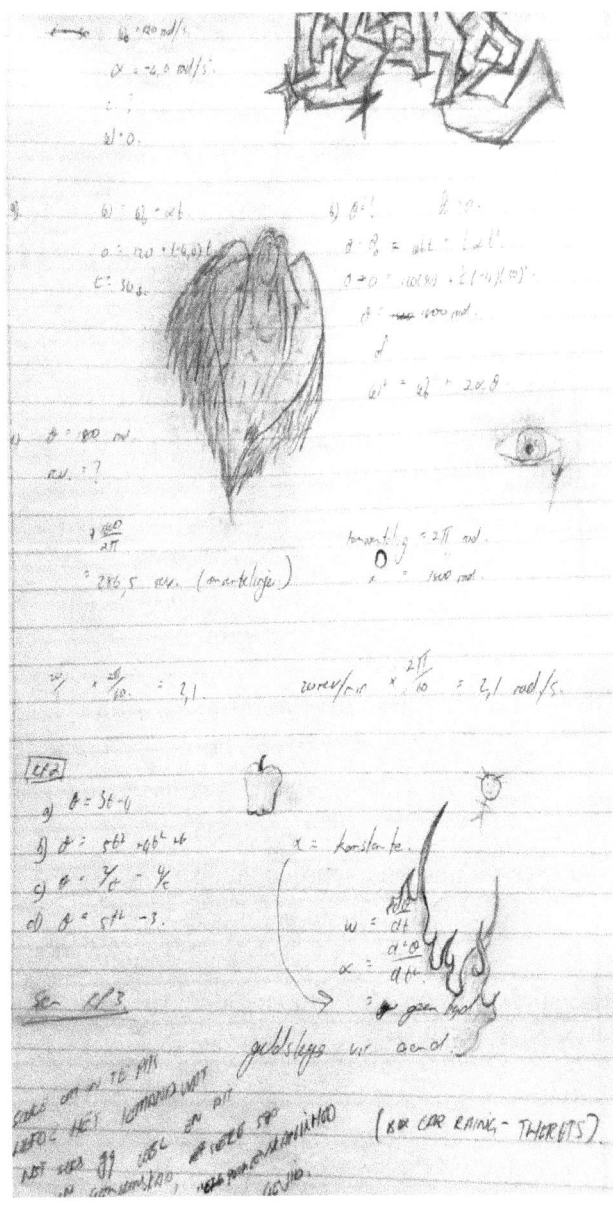

Seeing no way out, I became one of the marginalized peasants, a commoner, resolving to petty crimes to feed my addictions. I was feeling like little Oliver Twist looking at the puppet master Steven to save me from myself.

As I was seeking ways to escape from the circumstances that dominated my mind, I contemplated on altering my identity. Most superheroes have a hidden identity, and if I was to be the hero, I would have to portray myself differently. However this black hole that was sucking me into self destructive behavior of addictions, I was more likely to spawn a super villain instead of a hero.

A villain with multiple personality disorder...

This approach should at least give me some advantage, as I was working on a strategic plan on how to gain the upper hand over Steven. Like a chemical compound that can be destroyed by chemical means, into its smallest stable parts known as molecules, so I was being broken down through chemical means. And I was planning to experiment in ways to combine my most basic desires into a new form, and decided to formulate my new world views.

World views:

1. Love does not exist; it's an illusion to satisfy our carnal desire for sex.

2. Everyone has motives and hidden agendas, I have to expose them in order to manipulate people like a puppets.

3. No one can be trusted.

4. Never let anyone see the real you, only reflect the image they want to see.

5. Attack is the best defense, hurt rather than being hurt.

6. Never be driven by your own desires, but feed of the desires of other.

Maybe I was being over emotional, but I felt this is what is required of me at this point in life. After all I want to become a hero and there are some difficult decisions that a hero has to make. I have to toughen up and become a hard emotionless beast in order to defeat the enemy I am currently facing. With this new mind set I decided I was going to spend the night at Stephanie.

When I arrived at her place I saw Stephen leaving which ignited a fire of pure hatred within me. Not sure what to think I just enter her humble flat without saying a word. The rest of the evening the evening was filled with meaningless conversation, a few joints and a lot of coffee.

***

It was just another regular day, spent in the regular way on the bench between the physics, chemistry and biology building. I was sitting having a smoke, with the disposable cup filled with coffee on the bench beside me. The only thing that was different in this day was my company, as I was spending time with a friend named Michael. He was a pretty average guy studying accounting, but enjoyed sports, working out and the ladies, in essence a jock. I was observing the passing crowd as usual and Michael was rambling on about some girl he met at a party the previous weekend. Michael's voice became a stimulating beat allowing me slip into my own thoughts as I observe the crowds. As I drifted away, looking at an in love couple sharing a meal, laughing, and playing, I was struck with the human condition. The human condition, as described by Irvin D. Yalom in his studies as, people are concerned with meaning, loneliness, freedom and mortality, the indisputable features of being human.

The coupling sitting on the grass in the shade of a tree seemed to be cut off completely from the world surrounding them, capturing the answer to the human condition. This couple was defeating loneliness, experiencing freedom, and finding meaning in being lost in the moment, with absolutely no regard for mortality.

-"Are you even listing, man?" Michael said, snapping me out of my dazed state, back to reality.

-"Sorry, yeah, you were saying something about a girl." I said, hoping that he will not notice that my mind drifted.

-"Yeah, so do you think I have a shot?" He responded, with an excited look in his eyes.

It seems that my response was satisfactory, he was always rambling about some girl so I couldn't have been wrong, although I had no idea what he said.

-"Those who never try, never succeed, so you have nothing to lose." I responded with confidence.

-"You're right, like always!" Michael replied satisfied, seeming not to notice that I drifted away.

We sat a moment in quiet as Michael pondered his approach to capture the attention of the girl he recently met. Making use of the silence I slipped away into my own thoughts to further contemplate the human condition, and my opinions thereof. My thoughts lingered on the impact of this condition on our daily lives, and this might be the driving force behind various human actions. And it is at this moment that I remembered the words of William Shakespeare;

"all the world's a stage, and the men and woman merely players; they have exits and their entrances; and one man in his time plays many parts, his acts being seven ages."

This became an intriguing subject and I decided that I would spend some time to ponder the implications, observe those around me and maybe even make a study of this matter. My mind was like a steam engine that was brought into motion, and the longer it is running the more momentum it gains, until it is speeding along with such a tempo it hard to control. My thoughts were overwhelmed that this simple condition has influenced art, literature, music and maybe even the sciences and religion. It was at this point that I interrupted the thoughts of Michael with the words;

-"I have to go, I just remembered something, see you around man" and I got up and rushed home.

When I got home I immediately went and sat in front of the computer, and thought of the times that I was caught up with the human condition myself. This was a time in my life where I felt confused, alone maybe in even lost, and studied various religion seeking comfort. As I scrolled through the old documents firstly I was amazed with the collection of works that still remained, from Hinduism, to Judaism and Gnosticism, and even the pseudegripha. I was amazed that there was such a variety of doctrines, all providing some sort of explanation or escape from the human condition that so easily can drag us down into a pit of despair. It was then that I stumbled across some work regarding Zen as found its purest form among Japanese Buddhists. While reading through the work I read that '*a wise man turns his senses with his mind towards his heart*'. I paused for a moment to dwell on these interesting yet wise words.

As I ponder turning your senses toward your heart, I am reminded of the couple I saw earlier that day, and how they seemed to transcend the human condition. While the image lingers in my mind, my heart is compelled to believe that there is more to life than merely the human condition and that our heart and emotions plays an important role in this life as well. That life consists of love, and human relations, and that personality and artistic expression is a driving force for our aspirations. It was at this point that I considered the work of Karl Marx;

"It is not the consciousness of men that determine their being, but, on the contrary, their social being that determines their consciousness."

Karl Marx – A Contribution to the critique of political economy

And I realize that our social behavior can give away so much of our perspectives and believes…

Our concerns with meaning, loneliness, freedom and mortality, the human condition, can so easily become negative and surreal. But it can just so easily drive our search for understanding and beauty in science, art and literature. Humankind has come such a long way and has undergone various changes, from the reformation, to the counterculture and social revolution of the 1960's, and even our post modern times.

Our philosophies, religion, science and artistic expressions have undergone evolutionary changes over the year, and the process is not complete. This revelation inspires me and motivates me even more to embrace the human condition, and to be fully aware of my personal growth and change on this journey.

There is so much to live for, too much for one person to embrace alone, and trough our social behavior we share our stories of this journey contributing to the global evolution of society. By doing this we create our own revolutions and expression that become characteristic of our era, a legacy that future generation might envy.

Just like Kurt Cobain who became the voice of the teen spirit during the 1990's…

The following day I was at the University campus, as I usually spent my days. However today I visited a few different classes and not the usual, I attended some psychology classes, some philosophy and even an economics. None of these classes was in my field of study, however gave me some insights to my contemplations of the previous day.

I was making my way to the bench in the shade between the chemistry, physics and biology where I usually spend my time between classes. On my way to my spot, I stopped at the tuck shop because not getting coffee will be a break in my routine. It was not long before I was able to take my seat, sip my coffee and relax. As I sat back I lit up a cigarette, placed my head phones in my ears and took out my note book. As I started make a few sketches, the lyrics of Ben Harper rang in my ears, lyrics that seemed to coincide with my thoughts.

"They say time will heal the pain, I say pain is gonna kill my time…"

Ben Harper – When it's good

It was then that I looked up from my sketch pad, and noticed a familiar face in the passing crowd. I knew this face but for a moment I was not able to recall a name, or from where or why this person looked familiar. He was slender in build and was wearing washed out, torn skinny jeans, with a dirty and much wrinkled T-shirt of Guns & Roses. He was walking at a slow pace dragging his dirty sneakers on the ground and slouching his shoulders forward. His hair was long, oily and didn't seem too combed for a few days, he had ear phones in his ears, and the cigarette in his hand was burning out by itself. He didn't have a bag with him so I was not sure if he has been to class recently, or was just spending time on campus because he had nowhere else to go.

Considering my most recent thought on the human condition, I could not help thinking to myself that this young man seems to be caught in the full fury of this condition. It seemed that this young man has given up on his circumstances and lost all meaning and purpose, a troubling and humbling thought at the same time. It seems that no one can escape this inevitable human condition, and if we are not weary we will be devoured by it. As he looked up he seemed to be looking straight through me with emptiness is his eyes, and it was then that I realized this was Clive!

That evening at home as I was listening to some music I was haunted by the image of Clive, and I was thinking what can happen in a person's life to make them seem so…

Lost,

Hurt,

Helpless,

Confused!

I was not sure if I should feel sorry for Clive or try to help him. I realized that no one is safe, at some point in our lives the human condition will catches up with us. At some point in time we are all seeking for meaning, purpose, love and we realize we will not live forever and we need to make the most of the time that we have. Maybe Charles Darwin was right with his theory of natural selection, that only the strong survive and the weak will be devoured.

"It seems like everyday is the same and I'm left to discover on my own. It seems like everything is grey and there's no color to behold. They say it's over and I'm fine again, try to stay sober, feels like I'm dying..."

Saron gas (Seether) – fine again

Chapter 4: Rise of the phoenix

I was walking around on campus like a deranged man with no purpose, stumbling between classes, and just going through the motions. I started playing games in my mind, determining how I want the world to perceive me in the mornings when I woke. I would dress to match the image, and walk around on campus and look at people's reaction to see if my portrayal came across. I had my earphones in my ears as usual.

"Penny for your thoughts, but a dollar for your insights, a fortune for your disaster. I'm just a painter and I'm drawing a blank..."

Fall out boy – Don't you know who I think I am?

I stopped and took a seat on a nearby bench; I didn't have a usual spot anymore, so any old bench was fine. I took a seat and lit a smoke, giving no attention to people around me; after all today I was a philosopher. I was wearing a pair of shorts with flip-flops, a T-shirt with a long sleeve shirt over that. Half way through my cigarette I took out my earphones, and starting paying attention to the people around me.

Next to me on the bench was a well groomed young man, surrounded by a few of his friends. They were mocking him for saying something romantic to his girlfriend earlier, I assumed from their comments. This did not last too long as they were between classes and left, leaving their friend next to me on the bench. I took this opportunity to strike up a conversation, and maybe even talk about love...

-"Hey man, some harsh words there", I said with an inviting smile on my face.

-"Yeah, but it's just jealousy", he responded with a sigh.

-"Clive, by the way, so I presume you have a girlfriend", I asked politely.

-"Karl, and yes I do. How about you?" he asked to make small talk.

-"It's complicated, I'm not sure I have made up my mind about love yet", I responded hoping that this was an intriguing answer.

-"What do mean?" he asked with a confused expression on his face.

-"Well, I have experienced heartbreak, and I have experienced attraction, but I think love might just be an illusion. What do you think?" I asked and anxiously awaited the response.

 -"Well, love can cause us to hope and dream, and that feels good, but love can just as easily hurt and tear us apart. I believe there is some meaning in love and loving." He responded confidently.

-"I am not so sure about the meaning, but the rest sounds a lot like life." I said matching his confidence, and we both sat in silence for a brief moment.

-"Maybe life is about meaningful relationships?" he said breaking the silence. He started to fiddle in his back pack and took out a piece of shriveled paper and handed it to me. He said; "read this maybe you'll be inspired, I have to get to class. See you around man."

-"Sure, see you", I replied and started to unfold the piece of paper and read as he walked away.

Dihan Struwig

You didn't

Remember the day I borrowed your brand

new car and dented it?

I thought you'd kill me, but you didn't.

And remember the time I dragged you to the beach,

and you said it would rain, and it did?

I thought you'd say, "I told you so." But you didn't.

Do you remember the time I flirted with all

the guys to make you jealous, and you were?

I thought you'd leave, but you didn't.

Do you remember the time I spilled strawberry pie

all over your car rug?

I thought you'd hit me, but you didn't

And remember the time I forgot to tell you the dance

was formal and you showed up in jeans?

I thought you'd drop me, but you didn't.

Yes, there were lots of things you didn't do.

But you put up with me, and loved me, and protected me.

There were lots of things I wanted to make up to you

when you returned from Vietnam.

But you didn't.

-By anonymous

As he walked away with the words of the poem ringing in my mind, I was filled with a feeling of melancholy. I was thinking maybe, just maybe, life might be about meaningful relationships; after all I had this deep longing not be alone. Maybe it was better to have loved and lost, but still I had a desire to love and not loose, to be able to share my dreams and hopes, and not be judged. But the time with Stephanie was not satisfying at all; it was like we have become old friends in the retirement home. Not sharing meaningful conversation and if we say anything we snap and bite at each other like two caged dogs.

I remember some observations that I did a while ago with Slash, about science and relationships. Our observation was that two people can react with, and on each other, and the difficulty is to have the right people in the right reactions. Was it possible to break down meaningful relationships into such simple explanations, or were these explanations a way to give meaning to relationships?

These thoughts contradicted my world views that I recently established, and no matter what excellent explanations there where for these world views, I still had a longing for more, there had to be more to life? I established these views in order to protect myself from being hurt and disappointed, but it was not a cure for the longings.

I might not be a hero, just a vulnerable boy, with simple dreams, simple needs and simple aspirations but there has to be more to life…

The contemplations of a frantic mind

CHEMICAL EQUILIBRIA AND PEOPLE

Two chemicals react and produce product, and the reaction is reversible.

$$Ca^{2+}(aq) + 2HCO_3^-(aq) \longrightarrow CaCO_3(s) + CO_2(g) + H_2O(l)$$

And

$$CaCO_3(s) + CO_2(g) + H_2O(l) \longrightarrow Ca^{2+}(aq) + 2HCO_3^-(aq)$$

Thus

$$Ca^{2+}(aq) + 2HCO_3^-(aq) \rightleftharpoons CaCO_3(s) + CO_2(g) + H_2O(l)$$

Likewise

1 CEO + 1 people pleaser $\longrightarrow$ Flirtation + romance

And

Flirtation + Romance $\longrightarrow$ 1 CEO + 1 people pleaser

Thus

1 CEO + 1 people pleaser $\rightleftharpoons$ Flirtation + romance.

These thoughts were too much to deal with at this point in time, and I thought to myself that a joint will calm my thoughts for now. I cannot just light up a joint anywhere so I decided to make my way to the skate park. After all this was not too far from campus and I could walk there, and there, not too many people will ask questions.

When I arrived at the skate park I went and took a seat on the stands, and rolled myself a joint. I lit up my joint, sat back and just watched the skaters. As the effect of the drugs kicked in, I was amazed at how these skaters can fall and get back up only to fall again, and I laughed by myself.

It was not long before one of them needed a break and came to sit on the stands as well. He had a back pack with him and took out a cold drink and some cigarettes. As he lit up his cigarette and took a sip of the cold drink, I decided to start up a conversation with him.

-"Hey dude, how can you do this to yourself, the constant beat up I mean?" I asked with a slight chuckle and an expression of amusement on my face.

-"Well, you just choose not to look at it as failure, but practice", he replied exhausted.

- I laughed and said, "sure thing, but how much of this can you take before you quit?"

-"It's like this, without failure there can be no success"; he replied and took another sip of his cold drink. "You see, when you get on the board the first time, you might be a bit scared, and might fall. But when you get the courage to get past that fall you succeed in riding. With time you become comfortable with riding, and you considering trying a few tricks. Again you fall a few times, but eventually you get it right and that feeling is empowering. When you conquer the fear of a trick the thrill is gone, so you have to keep on trying new things, to better yourself, until you reached the place where you are satisfied with your success", he explained with confidence and all seriousness.

-"Cool man, wise words there, no failure no success"; I chuckled again and put in my earphones.

I sat back and allowed the drugs to calm my mind and allow the music to feed my soul. I took out my sketch pad just in case some inspiration struck me while I was sitting there, the lyrics rang in my ears.

"…I'm a brother with a furious mind, action must be taken. We don't the key, we'll break in…"

Rage against the machine – know your enemy

It was not long before dusk settled in and it was time for me to make my way home, after a productive day. On my way home I stopped off at the Dragon for a beer and to considering the happenings of the day. Afterwards I went home, and started my night time ritual of smoking a joints and watching Japanese anime before going to bed.

The next morning I woke up with a strong cup of coffee and a joint before considering my image for the day. Today I was going for the rebel look with some torn jeans, a pair of sneaker, dirty t-shirt and a leather jacket; I even went as far as putting on some eyeliner. After dressing I had another cup of coffee and a cigarette and loaded some metal music on my mp3 player before heading off to campus.

When I arrived on campus I thought to myself that there will be no philosophical nonsense today, after all emotions were for the weak. I was not in a studying mood yet, and it might take some time on campus for that feeling to settle in so decided to skip the first class of the day. After walking around on campus, it was about 10am, I decided to move closer to the physics building to drop in at a class. As I was strolling along I thought I heard someone calling my name, but as I had my earphones in and kept on walking. I heard the call again and took out one of my earphones to see if it was real or just my imagination. There is was again, and I looked around before noticing the guy with dreadlocks, long sleeve shirt with the sleeves rolled up halfway. He was wearing bootleg jeans and flip flops, it took me a while to notice it was Slash, and I walked closer. Like usual he had the disposable cup of coffee next to him on the bench and notebook on his lap.

I took a seat next to him and lit up a cigarette, before engaging in a conversation with him.

-"It's been a while, how have you been?" I asked bluntly with some irritation in my voice.

-"Been good, had a few interesting thoughts lately... How about you?" he replied hesitantly.

-"I have been through some things, but I'm surviving", I replied not engaging too much.

-"Sounds hectic man, but as long as your surviving", he responded.

-He always had some interesting thoughts, so I asked him; "what do think of the statement, there is no success without failure?"

-"Interesting statement, do have a few minutes?" he said excited.

-"Sure", I said as I was not very motivated for class, and this could waste a few minutes.

-"Rising out of failure is always inspiring and has been the topic of a few fascinating tales over the ages. It depends on the context of course for it to be relevant and inspiring, for example the underdog sports team or legendary heroes. One of my favorites is the stories of Hercules, in Greek mythology and the 12 tasks he had to perform. And the best part of that story has to be when Hercules travelled to the underworld, Hades, made it through and lived to tell the tale. A truly inspiring story of one man defeating death, and kind of reminds me of a phoenix as well. The phoenix is a mythological creature found in wide variety of cultures around the world. Is that answer good enough for now?" he said with a smile on his face.

-Although I didn't know much about the phoenix, I was not in the mood for an elaborate explanation, so I said; "yeah, sounds good, but I have to get to class, we should do this again."

-"That will be good, see you around man", he responded.

I stood up and walked away, leaving with the thought of the phoenix in my mind.

***

As Clive walked away I was thinking to myself that the hero image fits in nicely with my recent thoughts on the human condition and my readings on religion. After all not everyone gets to be the hero, but we all experience failures we need to rise from with our dreams and aspirations.

In these tales, the hero usually goes on some journey of self discovery, and realizes that fears are part of the deal. He always has some meaningful relationships, often a girl worth fighting for. But the most important quality of them all is a burning desire; I will even go so far as to say a holy dissatisfaction. This desire becomes the driving force, giving meaning and inspiring a fight for justice, to right the wrongs of the world, and to rise above circumstances, fears and failures.

These hero qualities to some extent fit a wide definition of religion...

Religion strives to not only give meaning to life, but for all of existence. It fills us with the hope that there is more to life, a reason 'to keep on keeping on' and to rise above circumstances. The believers or followers of a faith form a community striving to provide meaningful relationships. Religion then provides us with roots that ground us and give meaning, but religion also gives us wings to rise above and seek more.

These were such beautiful thoughts, so I decided to let them linger in my mind for a while. I sat back on the bench, took a sip from my coffee and lit a cigarette. It would have been good if Clive was still here so I could share these thoughts with him...

My recent thoughts have caused me to view things differently, and have even led me on a spiritual journey of growth. As I was sitting back, and taking a few moments to let my thoughts simmer, I viewed the people around me in a beautiful new way. I wanted to ask all of them about their own individual journeys and life experiences. Such a wide variety of people, and if I can find my own thoughts so inspiring, how much more inspiring would different perspectives be.

I spent the rest of the day, observing the crowds between classes, looking for incidents that portray hope and beauty. It seemed like the more I seek these inspiring moments the more they appear, almost like the law of attraction, which reminded of a song.

"Change will come, change is here. Love fades out, then love appears…"

Collective Soul – Reunion

A few days went by before I saw Clive again, and I was sitting in my usual spot with my usual routine, when Clive strolled by one day. This time I did not have to call him closer, he approached me on his own with two cups of coffee in his hands. He came and sat next to me, handed me one of the cups and took a packet of cigarettes from his pocket.

-After lighting up a cigarette he said; "good to be back."

-"Good to have you back", I replied, and we both sat in silence for a few moments.

-"Tell me the story about the phoenix", he asked politely.

-"Well, the phoenix is a mythological creature first of all, but is found in various cultures around the world. This bird has the life span of 500 to 1000 years, and at the end of its lifetime it builds a nest. When the nest is complete the bird ignites the nest burning itself and the nest to ashes. It is from these ashes that a new phoenix emerges, it like a fiery rebirth and the birds is believed to be immortal", I explained briefly.

-"I see, and you're a religious man, do you believe in a fiery rebirth?" he asked inquisitively and almost mockingly.

-"Now that is an interesting question", I said and paused a few moments before explaining my views. "I do believe that when you adopt faith, you begin a fresh start, and undergo some kind of rebirth, but not fiery. And further I believe that from that moment on a journey begins, and we seek knowledge and understanding in various ways. These ways can be through science, art, music or any other form of expression. After all if God created everything it's all connected in some way, and we try to discover this. Lastly I believe that inside us all there is something that connects us to God, some untapped source of potential. When we reach into that place, through meditation, rituals, prayer or any other means, we reach that place where we rise above, and inspire those around us. We are all heroes in our little sphere of influence, and religion is the way in which we are empowered."

-"That is some inspiring words man, I might even considering religion myself", he responded, and we sat in silence for a few moments.

- I chuckled and asked; "Do you require a rebirth of some sort?"

-"I am not sure if you should call it a rebirth, but I have been questioning life a lot lately", Clive responded facing the ground.

-"How are you dealing with these questions", I inquired politely.

-"I don't deal with it!" he replied with some agitation in his voice.

-Feeling that I have crossed some line my only response was, "ok".

-Attempting to change the topic he said, "I still have no idea what you are studying?"

-"I recently completed my studies in economics and for the past few months I have been employed by the University doing some admin work", I responded attempting to break the sudden tension. This was what I was doing at the moment however, and economics was not the only field I studied, life has a funny way changing our plans for us.

Like my friend I have also questioned life, love and everything else, and this has changed my world view a few times already, but I presume this is just part of the ebb and flow of life. Someone once told me that the music you listen to should change at least every seven years and through that you can know you are changing and growing as a person. I might be wrong but I feel that questioning life in this way is just part of the transition process from one stream of life to the next; you cannot change the course you're heading in if you do not question the current path. There have been some brilliant minds that walked the earth, each of them giving expression to their life experiences in different ways, and it is this expression that has inspired me on various occasions.

Chapter 5: The journey Begins

There comes a time in one's life where nothing seems to make any sense, like life has lost all meaning, and you feel stranded. A while ago it felt like you were rushing along in the river of life, overcoming rapids, twists and turns and maybe even crossing over the waterfall. And then all of a sudden it is as if you reach a quiet pool with clear water, surrounded by lushes' overgrown mountains, with no one else in sight. It seems peaceful and pleasant and in that moment it seems like the destination of choice, a place to settle down and make a life...

This feeling doesn't seem to last long as you realize that the stream is carrying you still on, and the peacefulness and tranquility seem to fade. You're surroundings change to a barren wasteland, and what was once seemed like a river seems nothing more than stream now. It is at this point that you question life, meaning, destiny, yourself and maybe even God...

The mystery and beauty of this is that you realize that there are no answers to life, there is no five steps to success, or a seven step plan to happiness. This is something you have to figure out on your own.

Alone.

It is then in the silence, alone and barren that you face yourself, your own worst enemy.

You face you're mistakes,

Failures,

Fears,

Successes,

Happiness,

Dreams,

Needs,

Aspirations...

It seems like this period will never end, and you fall into a depressed like state, unmotivated, uninspired, never sleeping enough. And just as you are prepared to give up hope completely, the rain comes.

At first the rain seems to be adding to the misery, but after a while it begins to bring new life, sinking in to every dry bone in your body. Every book you read gives inspiration, every song you hear sounds like it was written for you, everything taste tastes better and every smell is heavenly.

You start to dream again,

Live again as if life has a purpose!

And this is what it is all about, the ebb and flow of the river of life. Springing fourth a fountain of youth that those around can drink from and be inspired...

I guess that is why I am so gripped by the behavior of people?

All great stories include an adventure of some sort that stir up a variety of emotions and develops characteristic that could never have imagined. The great unknown may seem scary at first, as the tale progresses the great unknown becomes Fantasy Island. Every hero has his demons to face, and every damsel is awaiting her prince, all the land hungers to be concurred and treasures are waiting to be discovered.

I myself have been on a few journeys myself in my lifetime, and I have met strange and wonderful characters along the road. However the journey is far from over, and there is plenty of life to live, an in this point of time my companion is Clive. For both of us a journey is under way, and it seems like his stating to take a new path, while mine...

I am not sure where my journey is heading at the moment. All I know is that there will be many tales to tell when it is all over. All that needs to be done is to let the light shine, the light shines in the darkness and the darkness can never extinguish it.

Long ago before I existed, in fact before anyone existed, the word already existed. The word was with God, and through the word God created everything, and nothing was created except through him. The word gave life to everything that was created, and his life brought life to everyone. Then God sent a man to tell of the light, he himself was not the light but the light was to come after him. The word came to world and gave light; those that accepted were reborn - not with a physical birth resulting from human passion or plan, but a birth that comes from God. The word became flesh and he made his home among us. He was full of unfailing love, faithfulness, righteousness and justice. He gave rest to tired, and gave love to unloved; he accepted those who we rejected. He fought for the oppressed, and gave justice to those who have been trampled on.

His light shine till this day, and those who have seen the light can never be the same. They rise like and eagle from the nest, they roar like the thunder, and move like the wind. Sometimes they stumble and they fall, but their hope is in something more. They rise like the phoenix from the ashes, fight on and conquer, their light cannot be extinguished, and their souls cannot be tamed. They have a freedom that cannot be explained or taken away.

They live among us today, bringing hope and justice, to the barren wastelands that we so often call home.

They journey among us.

They might be us.

The roads leads somewhere for all us, for me and for Clive, and everyone I see every day. The questions that remain are who of us will be gathered at the end?

***

It was a Wednesday afternoon and I already had my morning joints and few episodes of anime when Steven arrived at my place. He came over to drop off some cocaine I ordered from him, since my downward spiral my dependence on chemical has escalated, I have tried various drugs since. I invited him in for a cup of coffee and a joint, as I thought it would be rude if he just came and dropped off the package. After the coffee and the joint he suggested that we hit a few lines of coke together. What started with a line or two ended up in us smoking some of the coke, a few more joints, more line and bottle of whiskey. With our minds and emotions numbed down to almost none existing, we ended up watching a movie, *fight club*.

"We're the middle children of our history, man. We have no great wart. No great depression. Our great war is a spiritual war. Our great depression is our lives. We've all been raised on television to believe that one day we'd all be millionaires, and movie gods, and rock stars, but we won't. We're slowly learning that fact. And we're very, very pissed off."

Tyler Durden – Fight club

After the movie ended Steven attempted to start a few mind games, but things have changed. I have grown and I have seen him in action as the master of puppets in the theater of the deranged. But I have found the secret to his power, and know how he pulls the strings, and if it was not for the chemicals he would be powerless. I have noticed that he has seen the power of drugs and he uses slight suggestions and music to alter the mood and determine the direction of the trip.

As I experimented with various drugs in this downward spiral, I have grown as soldier, and I am not stumbling from my previous wounds, I have become strong. I know the influence of the drugs I am taking and I know that I can control the direction of my own trip. He has no power over me anymore.

I must just be simple man, with my own aspirations, dreams and needs, but I choose my own destiny.

With these thoughts in my mind, I asked Steven to leave and suggested that he shouldn't come around anymore. I have no idea where my live is heading, although it doesn't look to good at the moment, but I know that it is far from over…

As Tyler Durden has said in *fight club,* our depression is our lives, and our war is spiritual. Maybe some of us are destined for a mediocre life, caught up in the same old time passing, time consuming rituals, that has bored generation before us. Maybe some of us are destined for a middle income job, married by 25, the average 2,5 children, and retirement at 65. The thought of such prospects fills me with a dark whole of despair in my gut. I was hoping and dreaming for so much more in life, but maybe I am the one that has to mediocre. I guess we need those kinds of people in life as well, I just felt that maybe I am special and gifted, and that my voice might change the course of history…

There is one thing that I know for sure, and that is that Tyler Durden was right. We surely are a pissed of generation, and maybe of lives are boring but at least we have a war. The war might be spiritual but I know that this generation is fed up with the way things are and the religions we have been taught as youngsters is not satisfying any needs.

These might be the signs of a revolution or a renaissance as we have seen in history. Our generation has seen and economic recession, unemployment rates are sky high, we have our religious determination. These were all factor that led to the previous renaissance, and the age of enlightenment. The scientific era might be coming to an end...

The answers that the modern era provided for lives biggest questions are not working.

This generation is calling for a leader! Some to challenge our existence, define our reality and give us a purpose again. I thought it might be me...

Life requires duality and tension, without the villain the hero has no purpose, and without the hero the villain has no cause. For a long period of time I have viewed Steven as some kind of wise sage that might lead me to become a hero, however like a chemical reaction he was part of mixture that creates something new. He was a particle that formed part of reaction in my being that is shaping me into something new. Before I was weak and needed a leader, but now, there is something else that is driving me.

Rage,

Hate,

Bitterness,

Greed.

"This state is elevating, as the hurt turns into hating.
Anticipating, all those fucked up feelings again.

The hurt inside is fading, this shits's gone way too far.
All this time I've been waiting, no I cannot grieve
anymore. For once inside awaking."

Korn – Here to stay

There is so much emotion inside of me at this stage on
my life, it feels as if the drugs are no longer having an
effect, or numbing them. Maybe it might be the drugs
that are causing these intense emotions, whatever the
case might be, it is exhilarating…

There is so much potential locked up inside us all, and
it takes a lifetime to discover this. Those people that
are truly exceptional are those that can mater this
potential early in life and that is a difficult task.
However there is so much to deal with in this life, and
how can we not allow these events to shape us in way
or another. I have been influenced by both Slash and
Steven recently and these forces are pulling me
opposite directions. Not only do these forces play a
role in my current worldview, but and to that my
current amplified emotions, and my perception as well.

Just like the circus can have a positive impact on
children, the image of the circus can so easily be

distorted into a morbid fantasy realm of the deranged. This image has been used various times to express hidden taboo fixations of people, with monster like clowns and horrifying laughter and a ring master that tames other worldly beast. This clearly illustrates the principles of physics I have been studying and even discussed with Slash on some occasion. These principles are the laws that govern our universe, and that is at least one thing the modern era has taught us.

Newton's third law: when a body exerts a force on a second body, the second body simultaneously exerts a force equal in magnitude and in opposite direction to that of the first body.

Our universe cannot function without a dualistic tension, so for every hero a villain is required. Change cannot come if we are not scared out of our comfort zones and forced to adapt in a new strange environment. This is the only way to separate the weak from the strong and change the course of history. Why do we as human struggle to find the meaning for suffering?

Suffering requires a source, just like change requires suffering. Suffering is a force, and it requires an opposite force equal in magnitude. On what other basis can our universe exist, function and progress.

Once upon a time there was light, but in order for the light to exist there had to be darkness. The darkness brought fear and uncertainty, and was consuming.

Once you were engulfed by the darkness the end could not be seen, for the darkness had no beginning and no end. Darkness gripped the hearts of a few men a struck with vengeance, they became the force dealt harm, pain and suffering on those deserving of such grief. But the darkness consumed these and it was not long before the pain and suffering spread to even those that where undeserving.

A battle began that last till this day and it was for the hearts of men, a battle between the forces of darkness, and forces of the light. But do not be fooled and under estimate the power of the dark, they might show themselves as forces of light in order to deceive. You see the forces of darkness have mastered the art of deceit and lies are their tools. They coming full op promises and bearing gifts, they might even promise you fame and fortune, but nothing in this life is free, I have seen for myself. Once you are hooked the road is long and alone…

ABOUT THE AUTHOR

Dihan M. Struwig is currently a theologian who pursues art and literature as hobbies, amongst other things. After completing High school he studied chemical engineering but could not complete this course due to his struggle with addiction. This was a struggle that started early in his life at the age of 13 and progressed to a dangerous lifestyle in his teens. His was able to beat his addiction through the Christian faith.

After beating addiction he began full time youth ministry and completed a Bachelors degree in theology during 2012. He plans to continue his studies and enrolled for an Honors degree in systematic theology which he hopes to complete during 2013. *'The contemplations of a frantic mind'* is the second book by this author and there are more in planning.

For more information on the author you can look him up through social media and the web.

)